T0246948

ISBN: 979-8-35093-348-2

Edited by Lowercase Editorial Services
Cover art and illustrations by Jordan Cloninger
Layout by Lowercase Editorial Services

Bigger

A Story of Forgiveness

By Tiffany Hall

Illustrations by Jordan Cloninger

See the girl looking out the car window? That's me.
My name is Alex.

Today, I'm moving because of my dad's job. He's a pastor
and we're on our way to a new church in a new town.

I ask Mom to be careful loading my favorite toy
horses onto the car. My brother annoys me by
making faces. As I watch my old house get smaller
and smaller, I feel nervous.

We arrive at the new house. Instead of unpacking my clothes and shoes right away, I take my horses out, one by one.

The spotted one is my favorite, but I love them all. I pretend they neigh and gallop around the room that smells like wet paint.

After a few days, my family settles into our home. While I'm playing in the yard, an older girl from our neighborhood stops by. Looking around at the moving boxes left on our porch, she notices my toy doctor kit. She says, "I know what we can do. Let's play doctor!"

I'm happy to have a friend,
so I say, "Yes!"

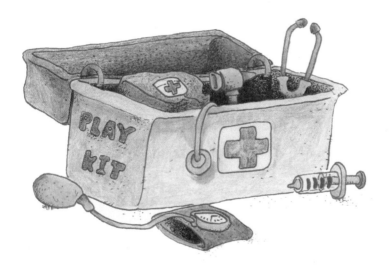

Playing doctor her way means I have to take off my clothes. It doesn't seem right to me when the girl touches my body—and where. I feel confused.

But she is **BIGGER** than me. If I tell anyone what we've done, the girl might stop being my friend. So I don't tell.

Over time, I forget about playing doctor with the girl in my old neighborhood. After a few years, my family moves away to another church in another town.

I sit behind my baby sister and brother. They sing silly songs as we pull out of the driveway.

As I hold my toy horses in my lap, I watch my old house get smaller and smaller. I feel lonely as we pass by our old church.

In the new town, my neighbor raises horses. When he asks me if I want to go horseback riding, I am excited. I love horses more than anything, so I say, "Yes!"

I don't like that he squeezes me tightly and touches my body, but he is **BIGGER** than me. If I tell anyone about his hugs, he might not let me ride his horses anymore.

So I don't tell.

Years go by. Another church needs a pastor. My family packs up and we move away. I leave my horses behind this time. Maybe some other kid will want them.

I don't even notice my old house getting smaller and smaller as we leave. It doesn't matter where we go. Why do I feel different than other girls?

As a teenager, I get to make more choices for myself. But sometimes I don't know what choice to make.

Do I want to date girls or boys? I'm so confused. I don't tell anyone about my thoughts and feelings. People might think I'm weird. Sometimes, I get angry and break things on purpose. Other times, I'm sad and cry into my pillow.

What's wrong with me?

Sometimes I talk to God, but I have trouble hearing Him. Everything feels **BIGGER** than me!

After years of pushing my old thoughts and feelings deep down inside, I've grown into an adult.

Look at me!
I've met a new friend who teaches me to rock climb. Ken is kind and adventurous. He's also cute. He doesn't ask me to do things that make me feel confused or uncomfortable.

We hike and camp together every weekend.

Our friendship grows.
He is the best friend I've ever had.
I feel safe with him.

But I decide not to tell Ken about the girl and a man who touched me when I was young. *God, it doesn't really matter, does it?* Besides, I'm afraid he might think I'm a bad person.

I keep my secrets to myself.
They still feel **BIGGER** than me.

Over time, I've learned to hear God speak quietly in my heart. One day, I hear Him ask me to share with Ken about what the girl and the man did to me.

At first, I'm afraid and nervous.

When I choose to tell Ken, he listens and gently holds my hand. Ken tells me he loves me.
It's the hardest thing I've ever done.

My secrets are out and I feel brave!

So why am I still angry and sad inside? I guess my feelings have been pushed down and trapped for a long, long time.
They still seem **BIGGER** than me.

I need someone to help me.

I choose a counselor who listens to me while I talk about what happened when I was a girl. She says that her office is a safe place to let all my angry and sad feelings out.

It's hard to talk about it, but I do it. I feel strong!

After sharing all my feelings with the counselor, I feel better. I understand that what happened was not my fault. But I still hate the girl and man. What they did was a long time ago, but I hope bad things happen to them. I wonder if I could ever forgive them. I think about it for a long time.

I ask my counselor what she thinks about forgiveness. She says I have the power to stop wishing bad things would happen to the girl and the man.

She tells me, "It's your choice *if* and **when** to forgive."

I'm worn out and tired of hating. Carrying hatred feels very heavy.

What should I do, God?

I decide to go to my favorite place and talk to Him about it.

God, I want to forgive the girl and the man.
I don't know how to do this by myself!
Amen.

God answers my prayer by showing me how to use my imagination to begin forgiving. First, I imagine my hatred is like a huge rock crushing me.

I can't get up with it on my back.

It's **BIGGER** than me!

What can I do?

God shows me that every time I wish bad things would happen to the girl and the man, I can take a deep breath and imagine letting the rock roll off. And every time I feel angry and sad, I can take a deep breath and imagine letting the rock roll off. My thoughts and feelings don't control me. I can control them.

I practice this way of forgiving over and over. Sometimes I don't feel like rolling the rock off. But after practicing for a long time, there comes a day when I'm ready to imagine rolling the rock off and leaving it behind.

Forever.

Choosing to forgive is the hardest, bravest, strongest thing I've ever done. I feel free and happy!

Because **BIGGER** than my secrets,

BIGGER than my feelings,

and **BIGGER** than my hatred...

my power of choosing forgiveness is the **BIGGEST** of all!

Throughout the story, Alex shows: loneliness, fear, confusion, embarrassment, sadness, anger, hatred, bravery, strength, and happiness. These pages are blank for you to draw a picture or write down how you feel or what you think.

Alex's story ends with a new beginning.
These pages are blank for drawing or writing
something happy that you would like to happen
for you.

What to Do
If Someone Is Touching You
in an Unsafe or Confusing Way:

1. *Say "NO!" to anyone who is touching your private parts.* This is called unsafe or confusing touch. Only doctors, nurses, and caregivers who are helping you are allowed to touch the parts of your body that your bathing suit covers.

2. *Get away* from the person who is touching you.

3. *Go to a trusted adult who will protect you:* a teacher, parent, caregiver, policeman, nurse, pastor, or social worker. Tell him or her what is happening to you. Use your voice until someone listens and helps you.

4. *Once you are safe, let a counselor help you.* Your feelings are important. It will take time to get your feelings out. It is okay to be sad and to be angry at the person who touched you in an unsafe way.

On Forgiveness

One day, you may decide to choose to forgive the person who touched you. You do not have to see or talk to the person to do this. It is your decision if and when you want to forgive. You can ask a counselor or someone you trust to help decide **what is best for you**.

Forgiveness does **NOT** mean that when someone touched you in an unsafe or confusing way, it was OK.

Forgiveness does **NOT** mean it is your fault you didn't say, "No!"

Forgiveness does **NOT** mean you should pretend what someone did never happened.

Forgiveness does **NOT** mean you have to remember all the details of what happened to you.

Forgiveness does **NOT** mean you have to trust or like someone who makes you feel confused or hurts you.

Children's Advocacy Organizations:

Darkness to Light | D2L.org

KAREHOUSE.org | (Haywood County, NC)

Keeping My Body Safe | channing-bete.com

National Children's Advocacy Center | nationalcac.org

National Children's Alliance | nationalchildrensalliance.org

NCChild.org (North Carolina)

PlayItSafe.org

Stop It Now! | stopitnow.org

Books & Resources:

I Said, NO! by Zack and Kimberly King

Your Body Belongs to You by Cornelia Spelman

About the Author:

Tiffany's curiosity to discover the best way to live a joyful life motivated her to write this book, as she believes healing and wholeness are possible for all. As a gardener and a chaplain, she delights in nurturing plants and people—witnessing astonishing beauty in both. Her home in the Great Smoky Mountains of North Carolina inspires her to lift her eyes unto the hills and find hope.

This story is dedicated to my family, whose love and faithfulness support my life's journey, and to Jesus, whose love and faithfulness guide every step.